This keepsake belongs to...

Text copyright 2013 by Eileen L. Ziesler
Illustrations copyright 2013 by Andrea Korpinen
Song copyright 2013 by Eileen L. Ziesler
Photograph copyright 2007 by Peter Olson
Photograph copyright 2012 by Susanne v. Schroeder

First Edition 2013
Printed in China

Book design by Andrea Korpinen

Summary: When the summer seeds have fallen and are covered with leaves
a hungry little chickadee seeks help from other woodland creatures.

Library of Congress Control Number: 2012955953

Ziesler, Eileen
    The Hungriest Chickadee:story / by Eileen L. Ziesler ; illustrated by Andrea Korpinen. -- 1st ed.

    Interest age level: 003-007.
    ISBN 978-0-9818831-6-8

chickadee...dee...dee

This book is dedicated to Meadow and her love of watching birds - A K

And to children everywhere who love and care for earth's creatures - ELZ

The Hungriest Chickadee

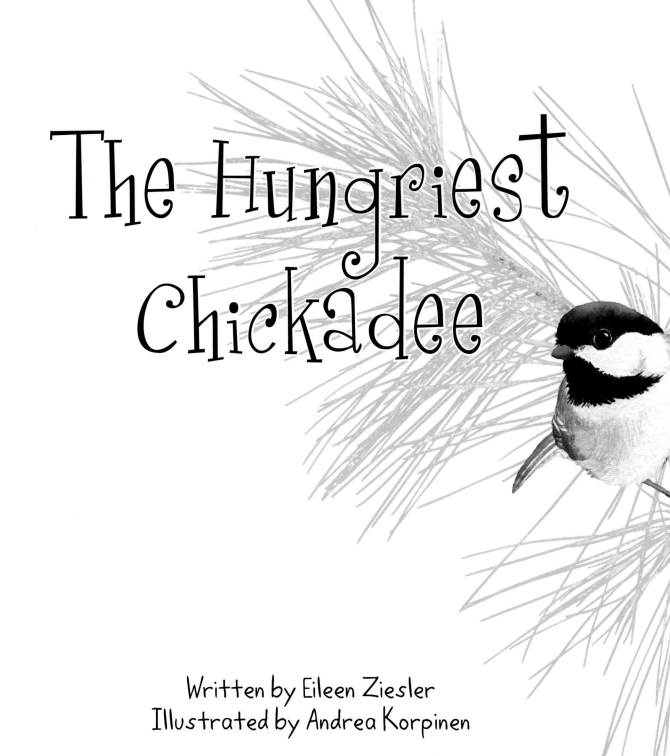

Written by Eileen Ziesler

Illustrated by Andrea Korpinen

In the green, growing summer,
seeds are to be found.

They grow on the grasses and fall to the ground.

The chickadees
find them
and eat!
and eat!

the seeds of summer, so lovely and sweet.

But when the leaves fall - yellow, orange, and brown,

they cover the seeds that lay on the ground.

"Have you any seeds?"
Chickadee asks of Gray Squirrel.

"No, no!" chatters Squirrel with a flourish and whirl.

My food is the acorn, so nutty and sweet.

Go ask Young Fawn, maybe she has your treat.

"Are there seeds on those twigs?"
Chickadee asks of Young Fawn.

"The seeds have all fallen, they have already gone."

"You might ask Raccoon to learn what he eats.

He might have what you need, some seeds for a treat."

"Are you finding seeds?"
Chickadee asks of Raccoon.

"No, no!" says Raccoon in the light of the moon.

"You might ask Black Bear before winter sets in

and he sleeps day and night in his warm cozy den."

"Are you eating seeds?"
Chickadee asks of Black Bear.

"No, no, little birdie!" growls the bear.

"I munch loads of berries before I sleep.

That's why my muzzle is sticky and sweet."

Chickadee flies slowly, cold, under his hood.

He's the hungriest chickadee that lives in the woods.

Who has some seeds this cold winter day—

The cardinal, the sparrow, or raucous blue jay?

Who has some seeds
for Chickadee to eat?

Seeds are so scarce
in the woods
dark and deep.

It is YOU! Little child with grandpa in tow...

filling the feeders that wait in a row.

And when you are finished, your grandma will make

warm chocolate milk and a little cupcake.

Then you can watch Chickadee eat! eat! and eat!

...the seed that you gave him, his own special treat.

You can make a treat for the birds so sweet....

What you will need:

Slices of dried out bread
Cookie cutters
Peanut butter
Wild bird seed
Yarn or string

What you do:

Cut shapes out of dried bread with cookie cutters. Spread peanut butter on both sides of bread. Dip both sides into a bird seed lined plate. Using a toothpick, push yarn through top of shape and tie to make a hanger. Hang them on tree branches and enjoy watching the happy birds eat! eat! and eat!

Can you name some of

Pileated Woodpecker

American Goldfinch

Mourning Dove

Red-Breasted Nuthatch

Chickadee's backyard friends?

Black-Capped Chickadee

White-Breasted Nuthatch

Blue Jay

Northern Cardinal

Song Sparrow

Downy Woodpecker

Andrea Korpinen

The End